Five re... ...we think you'll love this bo...

Winnie AND Wilbur
THE MAGIC WAND

goes
goes
...goes

Wir...
wrc...

The... much
to s... every
picture.

You get to see
Winnie's pants!

You can take the Winnie and
Wilbur challenge: how many
clocks can you find?

In this story Wilbur saves the day.

Freya

Anushka

Maggie

Bailey

Johannes

Molly

Ashley

Amber

Jun-Yeong

Pablo

Matilda

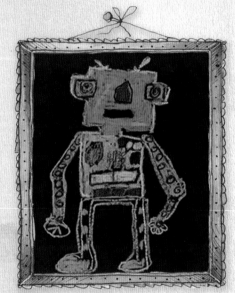

Marwin

Hasan

Rebecca

Winnie's Magic Wand is based on an idea emailed to Korky Paul by Mr John Fidler's Class Y2F, Akrotiri Primary School, Cyprus.

Thank you to all these schools for helping with the endpapers:

St Barnabas Primary School, Oxford; St Ebbe's Primary School, Oxford; Marcham Primary School, Abingdon; St Michael's C.E. Aided Primary School, Oxford; St Bede's RC Primary School, Jarrow; The Western Academy, Beijing, China; John King School, Pinxton; Neston Primary School, Neston; Star of the Sea RC Primary School, Whitley Bay; José Jorge Letria Primary School, Cascais, Portugal; Dunmore Primary School, Abingdon; Özel Bahçeşehir İlköğretim Okulu, Istanbul, Turkey; the International School of Amsterdam, the Netherlands; Princethorpe Infant School, Birmingham.

For Ron Heapy—V.T.

To Alexi—K.P.

OXFORD
UNIVERSITY PRESS

Great Clarendon Street, Oxford OX2 6DP

Oxford University Press is a department of the University of Oxford. It furthers the University's objective of excellence in research, scholarship, and education by publishing worldwide. Oxford is a registered trade mark of Oxford University Press in the UK and in certain other countries

Text copyright © Valerie Thomas 2002
Illustrations copyright © Korky Paul 2002, 2016
The moral rights of the author and artist have been asserted

Database right Oxford University Press (maker)

First published as *Winnie's Magic Wand* in 2002
This edition first published in 2016

British Library Cataloguing in Publication Data available

ISBN: 978-0-19-274828-7 (paperback)
ISBN: 978-0-19-274919-2 (paperback and CD)

10 9 8 7 6 5 4 3 2 1

Printed in China

Paper used in the production of this book is a natural, recyclable product made from wood grown in sustainable forests. The manufacturing process conforms to the environmental regulations of the country of origin

www.winnieandwilbur.com

Winnie and Wilbur
THE MAGIC WAND

OXFORD
UNIVERSITY PRESS

Winnie the Witch jumped out of bed.
It was a special day. It was the day of the
Witches' Magic Show, and Winnie was
making a wonderful new spell.

She felt nervous.
'I hope nothing goes wrong,' she said.

Wilbur felt nervous too. I expect something
will go wrong, he thought.

'What shall I wear?' said Winnie.
She got out her party dress.
Oh no! She had spilt red jelly on it!

Winnie threw the dress into the washing machine.
Then she threw in her towels, her pyjamas,
and her stripy tights.

She turned on the washing machine.
Swish, *swish*, *clunk*, it went.

When the washing machine had finished
going *swish, swish, clunk,* Winnie took out
the clothes and hung them on the line.

But her magic wand had been
washed as well. Oh no!
'I hope it still works,'
Winnie said.

Winnie dried the wand with a towel.

'I'll try it out,' she said. 'Something easy.
I'll change this apple into an orange.'

She closed her eyes, waved her wand, and shouted,

'Abracadabra!'

Suddenly there was an apple tree growing in her kitchen.
'Bother!' said Winnie. 'That wand's not working properly.'

Winnie dried the wand with her hair-drier.

'That's better,' she said. 'I'll try again.
I'll turn this apple tree back into an apple again.'
She picked up the wand, and shouted,

'Abracadabra!'

This time, the apple tree turned into an enormous apple pie.

'Oh no! **Oh no!**' Winnie moaned.
Now she really was worried.
It was nearly time for the Magic Show.
The wonderful new spell would be a disaster.

Wilbur was worried too.

Then Wilbur had an idea.
He ran out of the house,

MAGIC COFFEE MAGIC BOOKS MAGIC COMICS MAGIC FOOD MAGIC PETSHOP MAGIC CD-ROMS MAGIC FISH

down the road,

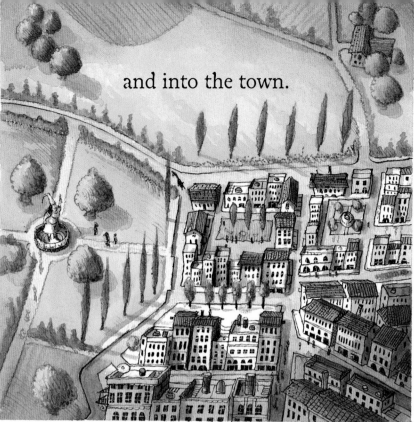
and into the town.

Perhaps *he* could find a new wand for Winnie.
He looked in all the shops.
But no magic wands.

Then, around the corner, he saw a little shop.
In the window was a big box of wands!

Wilbur grabbed one and galloped off home.

It was getting late.
Soon it would be too late for the Magic
Show. Winnie was very, very worried.

What could she do?

Then Wilbur ran through the cat flap with the new wand.

'Oh Wilbur!' cried Winnie. 'You are a clever cat.'

She didn't even have time to put on her party dress.
She jumped on her broomstick,
Wilbur jumped onto her shoulder,
and off they went.

They arrived just in time for Winnie's spell.
Everyone was sitting there, feeling excited.
Winnie always did something special.

'First,' announced Winnie, 'I will turn my
beautiful black cat into a green cat.'

She waved her wand, and shouted,

'Abracadabra!'

Wilbur waited . . .
Everyone waited . . .

Winnie tried again.

Nothing.

At last, a bunch of paper flowers popped
out of the end of the trick wand.

One of the witches started to laugh.
Soon everyone was laughing.
They laughed, they screamed,
they shrieked and fell off their chairs.

'What a clever joke, Winnie,' they cried.
'Where *did* you get that wand?'
Winnie smiled.
But she didn't say anything.

And neither did Wilbur.

Bethany

Katia

Eun-Jae

Kathleen

Ji-Eun

Jenny

Sara

Fraser

Ka Keung

Selin

Selin

Olivia

Siyabend

Kieran

A note for grown-ups

Oxford Owl is a FREE and easy-to-use website packed with support and advice about everything to do with reading.

Informative videos

Hints, tips and fun activities

Top tips from top writers for reading with your child

Help with choosing picture books

For this expert advice and much, much more about how children learn to read and how to keep them reading ...

LOOK
for Oxford Owl
www.oxfordowl.co.uk